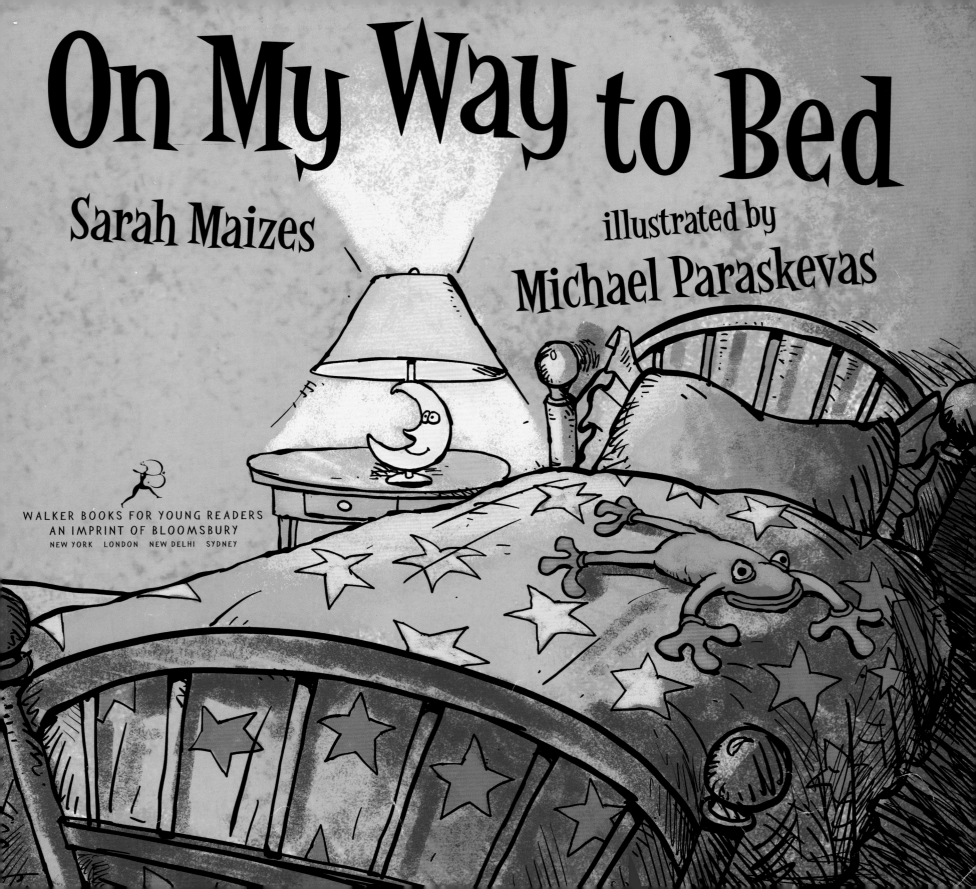

On My Way to Bed

Sarah Maizes

illustrated by

Michael Paraskevas

WALKER BOOKS FOR YOUNG READERS
AN IMPRINT OF BLOOMSBURY
NEW YORK LONDON NEW DELHI SYDNEY

First published in the United States of America in September 2013
by Walker Books for Young Readers, an imprint of Bloomsbury Publishing, Inc.
www.bloomsbury.com

For information about permission to reproduce selections from this book, write to
Permissions, Walker BFYR, 1385 Broadway, New York, New York 10018
Bloomsbury books may be purchased for business or promotional use. For information on bulk purchases please contact
Macmillan Corporate and Premium Sales Department at specialmarkets@macmillan.com

Library of Congress Cataloging-in-Publication Data
Maizes, Sarah.
On my way to bed / Sarah Maizes ; illustrations by Michael Paraskevas.
pages   cm
Summary: Livi imagines herself as a tightrope walker, a zoo dentist,
a magician, and more as she tries to avoid going to bed.
ISBN 978-0-8027-2366-6 (hardcover) · ISBN 978-0-8027-2367-3 (reinforced)
[1. Bedtime—Fiction. 2. Imagination—Fiction.] I. Paraskevas, Michael, illustrator. II. Title.
PZ7.M279540mm 2013   [E]—dc23   2013001363

Art created digitally with a Wacom Cintiq tablet in Painter and Photoshop
Typeset in Boopee and Latino Rumba
Book design by Donna Mark

Printed in China by C&C Offset Printing Co., Ltd., Shenzhen, Guangdong
2 4 6 8 10 9 7 5 3 1 (hardcover)
2 4 6 8 10 9 7 5 3 1 (reinforced)

For Ben, the best brother ever
—S. M.

For Judy, my twin sister,
who always makes me laugh
—M. P.

On my way to bed, I walk in a super-straight line. I do not fall over at all. I am in the circus—teetering on the high wire.

Don't forget to brush your teeth!

The crowd holds its breath as I perform daring feats! Watch me do a handstand!

On my way to bed, I brush my teeth. I help my brother brush his tooth too. I am a zoo dentist. I need to check the baby hippo for cavities. **Open wide!** Uh-oh. We might need to operate.

On my way to bed, I pass a towel on the floor. It is a cape, and I am a great magician. Abracadabra, I will make the piggies float. Flooooooat! FFFlllloooooogggggt!

On my way to bed, I see my sister working on her science project. I will help her. I am a rocket scientist and have been to the moon before. Froggolini is my copilot.

On my way to bed, I step over the pillows on my floor. I will build a fort, **WAY** up high in the mountains! I will live there with Froggolini. And a pet mountain goat named Marge.

On my way to bed, I swim across the ocean floor. I am an octopus. A big purple octopus! I use my suction cups to grab fish and food . . . and people swimming by. GOTCHA!

But I am not ready to sleep. I need a story. Hey! I am a teacher. I'll read you a nice long story. No, wait . . . **three** long stories.

A short one, Livi. It's late.

I need water. I am soooooooO thirsty. It's a desert in here!

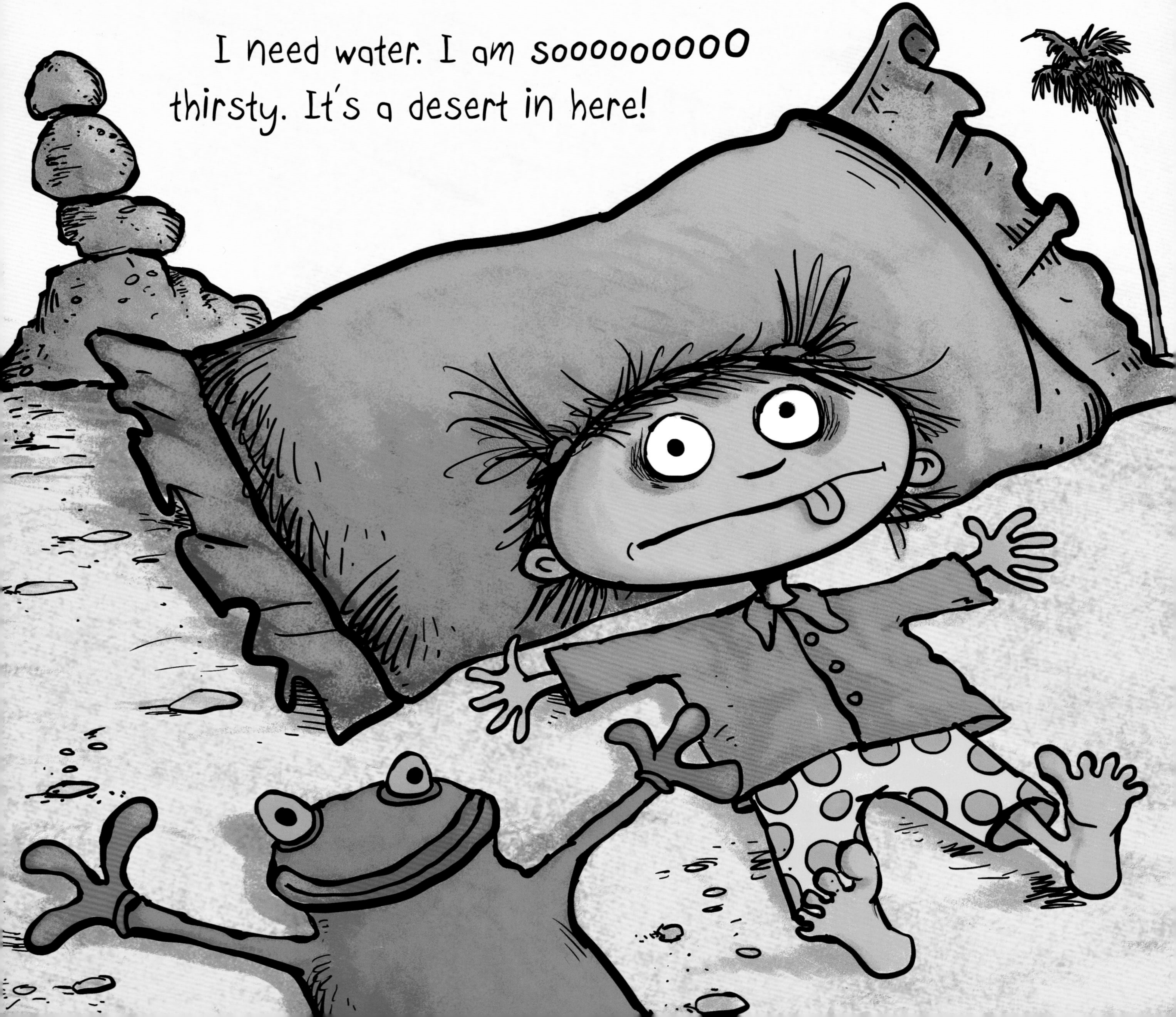

WAIT! I need the door open wide. Wider.
WIIIIDER! I don't want to miss anything!

I squirm, I snuggle, I sleep . . .